# My Funny Valentine

Written by Jon Colton Barry

Based on the series created by Dan Povenmire & Jeff "Swampy" Marsh

Printed in the United States of America     First Edition     1 3 5 7 9 10 8 6 4 2

Library of Congress Control Number on file.     ISBN 978-1-4231-2402-3

H886-4759-0-09305

For more Disney Press fun, visit www.disneybooks.com

Disney Press
New York

It was Valentine's Day, and Phineas and Ferb's older sister, Candace, couldn't stop thinking about the town dance later that night. She was going with Jeremy Johnson. She was so excited!

Candace imagined that Jeremy would show up on a white horse. He'd bring roses and stuffed animals and candy!

Meanwhile, Phineas and Ferb were trying to decide what to do that day. All of a sudden, they heard someone whispering.

"I need your help," the voice said. Peering out from behind the tree was Jeremy Johnson.

"I wanted to buy Candace a Valentine's Day present, but someone robbed all the stores and stole all the candy, stuffed teddy bears, flowers—everything!" he told them.

Just then, they spotted Candace walking into the backyard. Jeremy quickly hopped over the fence so she wouldn't see him. "Phineas!" she yelled. "You better not be planning anything crazy! It's Valentine's Day, and you *cannot* ruin it for me!"

Phineas watched as Candace ran back into the house.
"Someone sure is excited about Valentine's Day," he said. "Hey,
where's Perry?" he asked, looking around for his pet platypus.

   Perry the Platypus, aka Agent P, was standing in front of a large portrait of himself in the living room. He pressed a hidden button on the frame, revealing an entrance to his secret lair. Perry climbed through the opening.

"Good morning, Agent P," Perry's superior officer, Major Monogram, said from a large monitor. "Dr. Doofenshmirtz has stolen all the Valentine's Day gifts in the tri-state area. He is trying to destroy this holiday. You must stop him!"

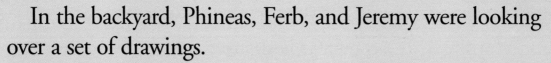

In the backyard, Phineas, Ferb, and Jeremy were looking over a set of drawings.

Just then, Isabella Garcia came by. "What'cha doing?" she asked.

"We're helping Jeremy with a secret project," Phineas said.

"Can I help?" Isabella asked.

"The more the merrier," Jeremy replied. "Just don't tell Candace. It's a surprise!"

"I promise," Isabella said.

Meanwhile, Candace was practicing her responses to all the gifts that she was hoping to receive from Jeremy.

"Oh, Jeremy, a dozen red roses! And all of these cuddly teddy bears! You *shouldn't* have," she said to herself.

Suddenly, she heard a loud noise outside.

Candace opened her window and saw Phineas and Ferb digging a massive trench in the backyard.

"Would you keep it down out there!" she yelled. "I am *trying* to get ready for the dance!"

"What's that?" Phineas shouted. "I can't hear you!"

"That's it!" Candace screamed. "I'm telling Mom!"

As soon as Candace left the window, Jeremy came out from his hiding place.

"Phew! That was close," Jeremy said with a sigh of relief.

At Doofenshmirtz Evil, Incorporated, the wicked doctor was admiring all the things that he had stolen.

"Look at all this heart-shaped junk!" he cried.

As Dr. Doofenshmirtz walked past a row of stuffed animals, one of them stuck out its leg and tripped him. It was Agent P! "Ah, Perry the Platypus, I had a feeling you were coming to see me," the evil doctor said.

Dr. Doofenshmirtz pulled a remote control out of his pocket and pressed a button. Just then, a stuffed bear leaned forward and clamped its arms around Perry. He was trapped!

"See, you weren't the only hidden surprise among the stuffed animals!" Dr. Doofenshmirtz shouted.

Back at home, Candace burst into her mom's room.
"Mom!" she yelled. "Phineas and Ferb are in the middle of a giant construction project in the backyard. You have to come and see!"

But her mom was busy getting ready to go out and didn't hear what Candace had said.

"It's almost time for the dance. Will you be ready soon?" she asked her daughter.

"You're right!" Candace exclaimed. "Jeremy will be here any minute!"

Outside, Phineas, Ferb, and Isabella were busy directing tanker trucks to the entrance of a long trench.

"Looking good!" Jeremy exclaimed. "We're almost finished!"

Back at Doofenshmirtz's headquarters, the doctor was explaining his evil plan to Agent P.

"I haven't liked Valentine's Day since I was a young man," he said. "That's when my true love broke my heart."

"And that is why I've taken all of the yucky flowers, icky chocolates, and silly stuffed animals out of every store in Danville!" Dr. Doofenshmirtz cried. "Now, *no one* will be able to celebrate Valentine's Day!"

"I am proud to introduce a new holiday to the world! It's called Broken-Heart Day," the doctor continued. "And with my new Fireworks-spell-inator, I will spell out *Broken-Heart Day* across the sky in bright lights!"

Suddenly, Perry broke free from his cage and thumped the doctor in the head with his tail. Then a major battle began!

"You can try to defeat me, Perry the Platypus!" the
doctor yelled. "But you won't succeed!"

Back home, Candace heard the doorbell ring. When she opened the door, she looked at Jeremy and frowned. She couldn't believe he wasn't holding any gifts!

"Candace, I'm sorry I didn't bring you a present. But check this out!" Jeremy pointed to a river in front of the house.

Just then, a gondola with Phineas and Ferb dressed as traditional gondoliers floated up to them.

"What's going on here?" Candace asked.

"Well, Jeremy wanted to give you a gift, and we wanted to build something cool," Phineas explained.

Phineas steered the gondola while Ferb played a song on the accordion. "This is one of my favorite instrumental pieces," Ferb said, speaking for the first time that day.

"This is really neat, Jeremy," Candace said, smiling. Jeremy smiled back. "It's not every day you get to ride a gondola through town! Pretty cool, huh?"

Back at Dr. Doofenshmirtz's headquarters, Perry wrapped wire around all the gifts and attached them to the fireworks. The evil doctor turned on the Fireworks-spell-inator. Perry and the gifts were immediately launched into the air!

"No!" Dr. Doofenshmirtz yelled as the fireworks exploded. The presents fell from the sky. Luckily, Perry parachuted safely away.

Everyone looked up as all the candy, flowers, and stuffed animals rained down on them.

"This is the best Valentine's Day ever!" Candace exclaimed. Then she and Jeremy headed into the dance.

Moments later, Phineas and Ferb spotted Isabella and Perry.
"Hey, guys," Phineas said. "Want to go for a ride?"
She and Perry hopped in and happily rode through town.
Once again, Agent P had secretly saved the day!